Marvellous Magical Stories

KINGFISHER
An imprint of Kingfisher Publications Plc
New Penderel House, 283-288 High Holborn
London WC1V 7HZ
www.kingfisherpub.com

First published by Kingfisher 2007
2 4 6 8 10 9 7 5 3 1

A CIP catalogue record for this book is available from
the British Library.

ISBN: 978 0 7534 1497 2

Printed in China
1TR/0407/PROSP/MAR/80NEWSP/C

SUPER SHORTS

Marvellous Magical Stories

Compiled by Elizabeth Holland
Illustrated by Sarah Horne

KINGFISHER

Contents

Chantelle, the Princess Who Couldn't Sing

Joyce Dunbar

Once upon a time there was a princess called Chantelle. She was as beautiful as she was good, as good as she was graceful, as graceful as she was kind. But the most enchanting thing about her was her voice and people loved to hear her sing.

When the princess reached the age of fifteen, a party was held in

her honour. All the guests came
with good wishes. All except one –
a peevish aunt who was jealous of
Chantelle. "Why should this slip of
a princess have so much?" she
grumbled to herself. And instead of
giving her a good wish, this jealous
aunt cast a spell so that when the
princess started to sing, her
beautiful voice was spirited away
and let loose out of the window.

"There," cackled the aunt.
"Sing away!"

From that day on, the princess could not sing at all. Not a high note nor a low note, not a la-la nor a tra-la: whenever she tried to sing, the sound that came out of her beautiful throat was flat, flat as a doormat.

"I can't understand it," said the queen.

"She used to have such a sweet voice," said the king.

As for Chantelle herself, it was clear from the way that she screeched and squawked so happily around the palace

that she simply did not realize. She had become completely tone deaf. The king and queen hired the best music teachers, but they all gave up in despair. And rather than offend her by telling her to be quiet, the king and queen and courtiers covered their ears.

Now it so happened that a handsome prince came to seek Chantelle's hand in marriage. He had heard all about the beautiful princess with the beautiful voice who so much loved to sing. But because no one talked about it, he hadn't heard that she could sing no longer.

As soon as the prince and princess met, they fell straightaway in love with each other and were betrothed. A celebration banquet was held and everyone ate, drank and was merry. It seemed there could never be a happier couple.

At the end of the banquet, the prince turned to the king. "Your Majesty," he said, "I cannot tell you how happy I am to be marrying your lovely daughter, so renowned for her lovely voice. You know that my court is famous for its music and as you can see I have brought my lyre. What could be a more fitting end to this occasion than that the princess should accompany me in a song?"

An embarrassed silence fell upon the court. But the princess wasn't embarrassed – not a bit. Smiling, she rose to her feet. The prince began to play and the princess opened her mouth to sing . . . but oh, what a dreadful noise she made – it was flat, flat as a doormat.

The prince stopped his playing in

astonishment. Then a page-boy began to titter, then a serving maid, until the whole court fell about laughing. But this was no joke. While the princess trembled and blushed crimson, the prince frowned. He could not possibly take such a princess as his bride – she would turn his court into a laughing stock! Muttering his excuses, the prince decided to return home. "I'll come back in a month," he said, "but make sure the princess has some singing lessons."

Poor Chantelle ran from the palace in tears. She found a hiding place among the bulrushes that grew by the royal lake and sobbed and sobbed, until at last a frog heard her and asked what the matter was.

"A handsome prince wants to marry me and he asked me to sing for him. But he didn't like my singing. Neither did anyone else. I can no longer sing a note," she sobbed.

"Don't you worry," said the frog. "I've a very fine voice myself. Meet me every morning at daybreak and I'll soon teach you to sing again."

And so, each dawn for a month,

the princess had singing lessons from the frog. She made excellent progress, and when the prince made his promised return, the frog told her she was sure to please him.

Once more a banquet was held, and this time the prince brought his lute. He plucked a few notes and the princess began to sing. But the sound that came out of her beautiful mouth was . . . well . . . a passionate, full-throated C-R-O-A-K!

Of course the whole court fell about laughing; all except the Frog King, who followed the sound from the royal pond and fell straightaway in love with the princess.

Again, the prince made his excuses, promising to return in a month, while Chantelle ran away in tears. She hid herself in a rose arbour and sobbed and croaked her heart out, until the kitchen cat came by and asked her what the matter was.

"I'm in love with a handsome prince who wants to marry me. But first I must learn to sing, as I can no longer sing a note."

"Don't you worry about that," said the kitchen cat. "I have the best voice for miles around. Meet me at moonrise each evening and I'll soon teach you to sing again."

And so, by the light of the moon,

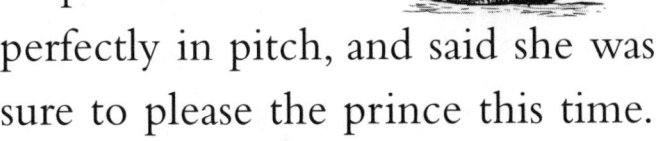

the princess had singing lessons from the kitchen cat. At the end of the month he pronounced her perfectly in pitch, and said she was sure to please the prince this time.

Well, you can imagine what happened. The prince began to play his flute and the princess started to sing. But the sound that came from her mouth was an ear-piercing, spine-shattering H-O-W-L!

And the court laughed until their sides ached. The prince did not laugh but departed as before, vowing

that he would give the princess
only one more chance. And the
King of Cats did not laugh either.
He followed the sound from the
other side of a forest and fell
straightaway in love with her.

This time the princess ran away
to a wood where she could cry
her heart out in peace. But she
woke up an owl, who asked her
what the matter was.

The princess told her story.

"We'll soon put that right," said the owl. "I've got a voice that charms the birds off the trees. Meet me at midnight every night and I'll soon teach you to sing once more."

So every midnight in the wood the princess took singing lessons from the owl.

"There," said the owl at last. "You too can charm the birds off the trees. You should certainly be able to charm a prince."

At the next banquet, when the princess opened her beautiful mouth to sing, the sound that came from her throat was the shrillest, sharpest TOO-WHIT-TOO-WHOO!

Although they tried to stop themselves, everyone fell off their chairs, howling and hooting with laughter. They laughed until the tears rolled down their cheeks, cruel tears of mockery. How the princess blushed! How humiliated she felt!

But the Owl King in the forest heard her and fell straight off his treetop in love.

This time the princess ran so far into the dark forest that she was lost. Now this part of the forest was enchanted, and it was here that the princess, worn out with misery and hunger, fell asleep.

The Frog King eyed her from an

enchanted pool. The King of Cats gazed at her from beside an enchanted stone. The Owl King blinked at her from an enchanted tree.

Then a strange sound began, a clear and beautiful sound. It was a human voice! It sang so finely and so sweetly, a melody as light as air, that it woke up the princess.

Although Chantelle did not know it, it was her own voice. Stolen by the peevish aunt and let loose out of the window, the voice had sung its way to the enchanted forest. Now it worked its charm on the princess and she could hear truly again.

"Oh, I would give everything to have a voice like that," sighed the princess.

"Be mine and you shall!" croaked the Frog King, wishing she was a frog.

"Be mine and you shall!" howled the King of Cats, wishing she was a cat.

"Be mine and you shall!" hooted the Owl King, wishing she was an owl.

In that instant the lovely voice was hers again. But in this enchanted forest, wishes had a dangerous way of coming true. As she sang, she changed. She lost her human form. Instead, she was the colour of a frog, with the fur of a cat and the shape of an owl! Only her eyes were her own.

The Owl King screeched in
dismay, the Frog King croaked in
disgust and the King of Cats slunk
away in distaste. When Chantelle
went to drink in the enchanted
pool, she wept to see what she
had become.

Now she could sing better than
any human being alive, to the lyre,
to the lute and the flute. But what
prince would want her now? What
use would she be to anyone? With
her own wings she soared through
the forest, her singing more
beautiful by day than the lark's,
more beautiful by night than the
nightingale's.

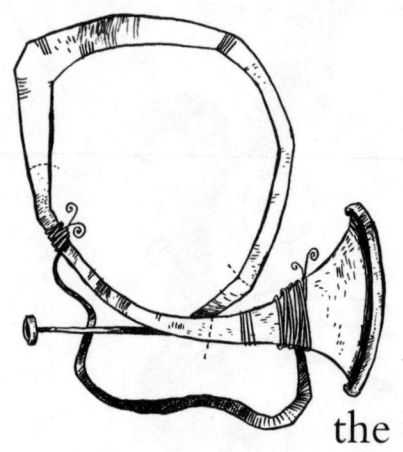

It so happened that the very same prince went hunting with his men in the forest one day. He was full of remorse at the disappearance of Princess Chantelle and had given up hope of finding her. So, when he heard this beautiful voice he made a vow.

"I gave up the princess I loved for a voice," he said to his men. "Now, here is a beautiful voice. Whoever owns it, whether she is young or old, wise or foolish, fair or foul, I will marry her. Catch her by whatever means you can." And because it was an enchanted forest, where wishes came strangely true, the huntsmen caught Chantelle in the first trap they set and brought her before the prince, so changed that he did not know her.

She sat in a gilded cage, singing and singing, a creature so weird and wonderful that the prince could only stare at her in appalled fascination. But a prince must keep his word. Without further ado, he married the strange creature and took her back to the palace.

But she did not sit on the throne as his princess.

Instead she was locked in
a tower at the very top
of the palace, there to
sing her heart out,
filling the palace and
its grounds with her
beautiful melodies.
The prince listened
and was enchanted,
for in the sound
was a vision of the
beautiful Princess
Chantelle.

"If only I had
married her,"
he kept saying
to himself.

"How happy I should be. But I asked for everything. So now I have my just rewards. I am married to a voice — nothing but a voice. I have to make the best of it."

Because the prince could not bear to look at the strange creature, he hired a keeper to take care of her. And it happened that this keeper was none other than the peevish aunt who had cast the spell on the princess. She recognized the eyes and the voice of Chantelle and she had an evil thought.

"What a waste of a handsome prince! What a waste of a beautiful voice! If only I could steal the voice for myself the prince might marry me instead. But first I must get rid of this monster."

She fed poisoned food to the strange creature, day after day, little bit by little bit, until at last the creature fell into a deep sleep from which nothing could awaken it.

"We must take it back to the heart of the forest where we found it," said the prince. "There, it might revive."

They went in solemn procession, the princess carried on a bier to the middle of the enchanted forest, the peevish aunt keeping watch.

"One last dose of poison," she said to herself, "and all that is hers shall be mine."

But the Owl King in his treetop heard her. The Frog King on his lily pad heard her. The King of Cats in the undergrowth heard her.

"You want what the princess has," they said, "and you shall have it!"

Because this was a place where wishes had a dangerous way of coming true, no sooner was this uttered than the strange creature turned back into Princess Chantelle, as warm and alive and human as on the last day the prince had seen her. At the same time the peevish aunt's neck began to bulge like a frog's, her voice began to hiss like a cat's and her face became as sharp as an owl's. She screamed with rage and tore through the forest, never to be seen again.

The prince looked at his beloved princess and said, "What a fool I have been. Can you ever forgive me?"

Princess Chantelle did forgive him, and when she opened her mouth to sing, the sound that came out of her beautiful throat was the voice that had been let loose in the enchanted forest. It was her own true voice, so happy to have found its owner that it la-laad and tra-laad as merrily as could be.

The Magical Apple Tree
Judy Hindley

Rosy lived with a mean old wicked witch. The witch did nothing at all but count her money. Rosy did all the work.

She fed the hens that laid eggs for the witch.

She fed the cow that gave milk to the witch.

She fed the horse that pulled the cart that carried the wood for the witch's fire.

All summer she grew corn and hay and oats to fill the barns for the animals' winter food.

But the witch sold the corn and hay and oats and kept the money.

When winter came, there was no food in the barns.

The hens were so hungry they laid no more eggs.

The cow was so hungry it gave no more milk.

And the poor old horse was too weak to pull the cart.

The witch said, "YOU'RE NO USE, NOW.

"Tomorrow morning the hens will go in the cooking pot and the cow will go to the butcher.

"That old horse can go wherever it likes – and so can you!"

She kicked Rosy out into the snow and slammed the door. Then she laughed her wicked laugh, "Caw, caw, caw!" just like a mean old crow.

Rosy cried, but the hungry animals gathered around her.

So she said, "I must go on. After all, crying won't help, and trying might help." She picked up her empty basket and went away into the cold, bare woods.

Rosy walked and walked till she came to an apple tree. It called to her. In a sad little voice it cried, "Please, dear Rosy, shake me, shake me, or this heavy fruit will break me!"

Rosy looked up. All she saw was one dead leaf. But the tree cried, "Shake me, shake me!" So she did.

Suddenly, it was covered with yellow apples! Rosy filled her basket and hurried home.

As she went, the basket got heavier and heavier.

But she didn't stop for a minute till she got home.

She tipped out the fruit and the animals crowded around.

None of them saw that the last five apples had turned to gold.

But the witch did. "AHA!" she cried. "WHO DID YOU ROB?"

"No one," said Rosy. "I found

these apples in the woods. There were lots and lots."

"LOTS?" cried the witch. And she rushed into the woods.

Through the bare trees, the magical apple tree glimmered with fruit.

But the witch pushed past.

"Please," cried the apple tree, "shake me, shake me, or this heavy fruit will break me!"

But the witch said, "Pooh! I'm looking for golden apples. Shake yourself!"

So it did.

But this time, the apples turned into stones.

"Ow, ow, ow!" cried the witch. She hopped and flapped, just like a mean old crow.

And suddenly the wind picked her up and whirled her away. And she never came back.

But Rosy sold the golden apples and was rich! And she and the animals never went hungry again.

The Three Wishes

The Brothers Grimm

There was once a poor man who had a very pretty wife. They were so poor that they had hardly enough to eat and hardly enough wood to make a fire. But one winter evening the man came in with a shiny brass coal scuttle, piled high with coal. "Look what I found by the door," he said to his wife. "It must be a gift. We shall have a good blaze tonight."

They sat
down to warm
themselves and
the wife began to
talk about the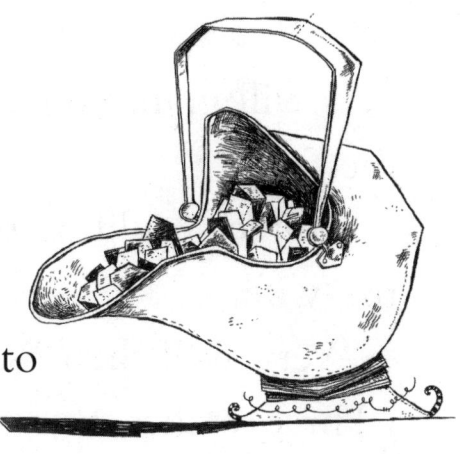
neighbours. "They are happier than
we are because they are richer," said
the wife. "But if only we could
meet a fairy, who would grant us a
wish, we should be happier and
richer than all of them."

"That would be a fine thing," said
her husband.

No sooner had they spoken than
a fairy fell from the embers of the
glowing fire.

"I will grant you a wish," said the fairy.

"Three would be better," said the wife.

"Very well then," said the fairy. "Three wishes. But only three wishes. I will grant you nothing more." And with that, she faded away.

The man and his wife settled down to decide what to wish for. "I will not make a wish yet," said the wife, "but I think nothing could be

better than an embroidered silk purse, full of gold."

"What a silly wish," said her husband. "Why, you could wish for ten silk purses, twenty, or even a hundred. But what use would they be to you if you were sick? It would be much better to wish for health, happiness, and a long life."

"But what is the use of a long life if you are poor? It only makes the misery last longer. Now I come to think of it, that fairy should have granted us a dozen wishes. Then we could have everything we want."

"That's true," said her husband. "But never mind. If we take our time and think carefully, we will make the most of our three wishes."

"I will think all night and make up my mind in the morning," said his wife. "Meanwhile, let us warm ourselves by the fire, for it is very cold." She poked the fire until it flared up very nicely, but her tummy rumbled with hunger. "Ah," she sighed, without thinking. "What a splendid fire. I wish we had a length of black pudding to cook on it for our supper."

She had hardly said these words when clitter-clatter down the chimney came a length of black pudding, more than enough for two.

Her husband was furious. "You greedy guts!" he shouted. "Blow you with your black pudding! What a waste of a good wish! Why, I wish that black pudding was fastened to the end of your nose!"

He soon felt sorry he had spoken, for the black pudding jumped up immediately and stuck fast on the end of his pretty wife's nose.

"Owwww! What have you done?" wailed the wife. "Get it off!"

Her husband gave it a pull, but it stuck. Then she gave it a pull, but it stuck. Then they both pulled so hard that they nearly pulled her nose off, but it was really, really stuck.

"I'm sorry, wife," said the husband. "But what if I were to wish for that embroidered silk purse, after all? You could use it to hide the black pudding."

"Owwww!" wailed the wife. "I should hide my head in that coal scuttle. How could I bear to be seen with a black pudding dangling from the end of my nose, even with a silk purse to hide it? Oh, I do wish it would drop off."

That very instant, the black pudding dropped off the wife's nose.

"There goes our last wish," groaned her husband.

"Owwww! Owwwww! Owwwww!" wailed the wife.

But she sat down and thought for a while, until at last she came to her senses. "It serves us right. We asked for too much and this is how the fairy has punished us. From now on we should count our blessings. See! We have a shiny brass coal scuttle half full of coal. We have a black pudding. That is more than we had to begin with.

Why don't we sit here by the warm fire and cook the black  pudding for our supper?"

And they did. And oh, it was good.

The Cletterkin

Jenny Koralek

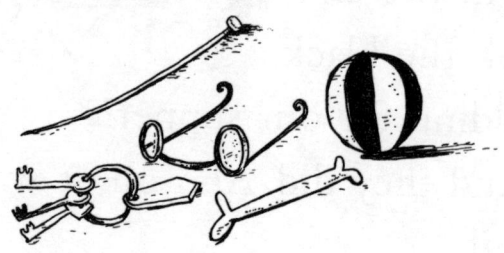

One morning after breakfast, Leggie Meggie ran into the garden to play with her new, yellow, very small bouncy ball. And after one bounce she lost it. She rushed indoors calling, "Mum! Dad! Grannie! I've lost my new best ball!"

"I can't help you now," said Dad crossly. "I've lost my car keys. I will have to walk to work and I'll be

very late."

"What we need in this house," said Grannie, "is a cletterkin."

But Dad didn't hear. He had gone, banging the door behind him.

"And I can't help you," said Mum. "I've lost my glasses. I've hunted high and low. I won't be able to read my book on the way to work, and I'll be late too."

"What we need in this house," said Grannie, "is a cletterkin."

But Mum didn't hear. She had gone, banging the door behind her.

Leggie Meggie heard, though.

"What's a cletterkin?" she asked.

Grannie looked up from her knitting. "A cletterkin finds things," she said. "And tidies what's untidy. A cletterkin can see into all the little nooks and crannies, indoors and out, where balls roll and car keys fall and glasses lie. When I was a girl every house had a cletterkin."

"What does a cletterkin look like?" asked Leggie Meggie. "I've never seen one myself," said Grannie.

She stopped to pick up a stitch from her knitting, "but . . . "

"But what?" asked Leggie Meggie.

"Once I met a man who'd met a man who said . . . a cletterkin has furry feet and leafy hair. He moves on feet as soft as cats' paws. He can shoot up as tall as a tree and shrink as small as a mouse. And because he can hunt high and low, he can find high and low. I never saw the cletterkin in our house, but I know, I just know he was the one who always found my lost pocket-money penny and my brother's best blue marble."

"What was that noise?" asked Leggie Meggie.

"What noise?" said Grannie.

"Soft on the floorboards, like cats' paws," said Leggie Meggie.

"I heard nothing," yawned Grannie. "And now, oh dear, I've lost my knitting needle. I tell you, what we need in this house is a cletterkin."

She yawned again and began to nod off in her chair.

Leggie Meggie went back into the garden to look for her ball. She looked in the long grass. She looked under the bushes. She fetched a stick and poked about in the stinging nettles. Where could it be?

"Perhaps it fell into one of the

flowerpots,"
she said.
She looked
in three
flowerpots.
They were
empty, except
one which had

a little bed of dry leaves
and some snail shells full of
raindrops. She was just about to put
her hand into another flowerpot
when a voice said:

"Didn't you know, long-leggedy,
it's very rude to scrabble about in
people's houses? You've just unmade
my bed and tipped over my cups."

There, by the flowerpot with the bed of dry leaves and the snail shells full of raindrops, was a little man with leafy hair and furry feet. He was sitting on Leggie Meggie's new, yellow, very small bouncy ball.

"A cletterkin!" cried Leggie Meggie. "Just like Grannie said!"

"Not a cletterkin," said the little man. "*The* cletterkin, the last cletterkin."

"What happened to the others?" asked Leggie Meggie.

"They went away long ago to look for the rainbow's end," said the cletterkin.

"Oh dear," said Leggie Meggie.

"They'll never find it."

"I know," sighed the cletterkin.

"Don't be sad," said Leggie Meggie. "We need you in our house. Grannie says so, because we're always losing things. Just in one morning I've lost my ball, Dad's lost his car keys, Mum's lost her glasses and Grannie's lost her knitting needle! Oh, won't you be our cletterkin?"

"Well," said the cletterkin briskly, "you do sound like a very untidy family!" But he made that sound like something good. "If you've lost all those things since you got up this morning, who knows what you'll have lost by bedtime? I'd better get started straightaway."

So Leggie Meggie led the way into the house. She showed the cletterkin the cat-flap.

"You can always come in and out through there," she whispered, "when I'm not here to let you in. Because we will be secret about you, won't we?"

"Of course," said the cletterkin, "and anyway, I have a little trick. I can make myself invisible if I want to."

"Go on then," said Leggie Meggie. Suddenly the cletterkin had vanished, but Leggie Meggie heard his voice singing, "Cletter cletter, that's better!" Then something

scuttled through the newspaper lying like a tent on the floor – and there were Mum's glasses lying at Grannie's feet.

"Cletter cletter, that's better," came a voice from somewhere near the front door. "Car keys in an old wellie! There's enough work here for a hundred years."

There was a scurrying of feet as soft as cats' paws, and there were Dad's keys lying at Grannie's feet.

"Cletter cletter, that's better," sang the invisible cletterkin, and Grannie's knitting needle seemed to heave itself up from a wide crack in the floorboards.

And there he was, sitting on top of Grannie's wool basket.

Just then the door banged and

Leggie Meggie heard her mother calling.

"I must go now," she said.

"And I'm off to my house," said the cletterkin.

"I'll come out and play later," whispered Leggie Meggie, and the cletterkin shot out through the cat-flap.

When Mum and Dad saw all the lost things laid out at Grannie's feet, they were very pleased.

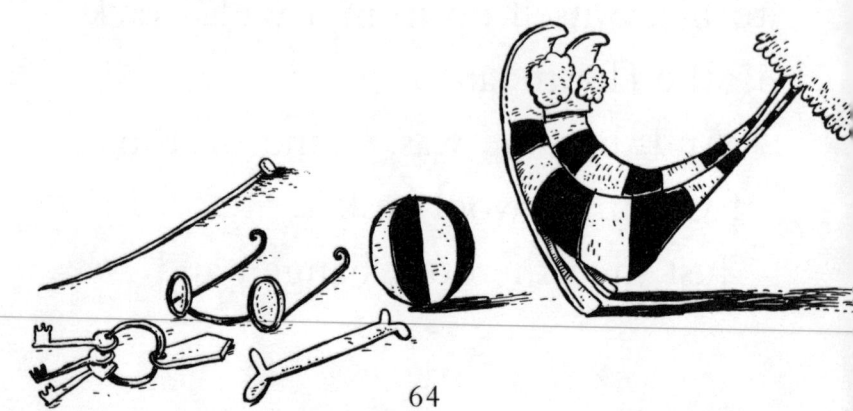

"Good girl, Leggie Meggie," said Dad.

"It wasn't me," said Leggie Meggie.

"Was it Grannie then?" They smiled at Grannie sleeping in her chair. "Dear Grannie, no wonder she's tired."

Then Grannie woke up. She saw her lost knitting needle neatly placed beside her wool. She saw Leggie Meggie holding her new, yellow, very small bouncy ball. She saw the keys and Mum's glasses lying by her feet.

"Well," she said. "Perhaps there is a cletterkin about after all!"

The Wonder Broom

Joyce Dunbar

Philipippa was the kitchen maid in King Carraway's palace. She washed the Royal Dishes, peeled the Royal Potatoes and swept the Royal Floors.

She did a lot more work besides, for the Royal Cook was a bully, who never stopped bossing her about.

The Royal Cook was also very fat. Her cotton print dresses were so tight that it looked as if the buttons might burst at any moment.

One morning, the Royal Cook sent Philipippa to the market to buy a new broom. "This old one is disgusting, a disgrace to the Royal Household," she said crossly.

"Yes, Ma'am," Philipippa answered politely.

It didn't take Philipippa long to walk there. She tried every stall but she couldn't find a broom anywhere.

She didn't dare go back to the Royal Palace without one, for then the cook's buttons would surely burst.

She was wondering what to do when a pedlar came by. "Wonder brooms! Wonder brooms!" he shouted.

"But you have only one broom," said Philipippa.

"Why yes. These brooms are so wonderful that I have sold all the others," lied the pedlar. "This is the last one I have left." He didn't tell her that he had found just that one broom on the Royal Road that very morning!

Philipippa bought the wonder broom and hurried back to the Royal Palace.

"Dawdler! What a time you've been!" the cook scolded.

"Indeed, Ma'am, I—"

"Enough of your cheek!" snapped the cook. "And don't just stand there gawking. Anybody would think we had nothing to do!

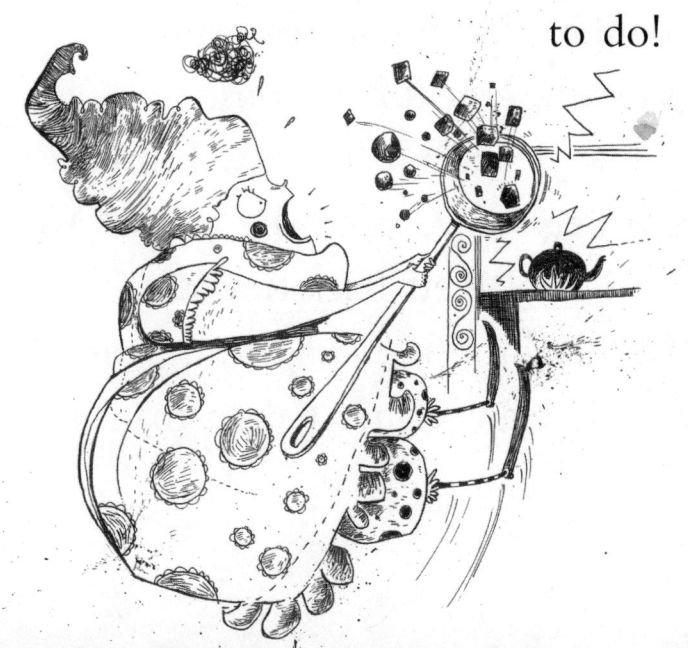

I've been making the stuffing for
the Royal Goose and the crumbs
have gone all over the floor. Sweep
the kitchen! Sweep the hall! Sweep
the yard!" With that, the cook
snatched up a Royal Saucepan and
banged it down on the fire so hard
that hot coals shot off in all
directions.

"My! What a temper she's got,"
thought Philipippa, nervously
watching out for buttons.

She picked up the new broom
and began sweeping the floor. Over
the Royal Red Tiles flew the
wonder broom, *swish, swish, swish.*
She had no sooner begun than it

was done. Not a crumb nor a hot coal in sight! Philipippa stared in amazement. It really was a wonder broom. So light! It must be enchanted.

"Well, if this isn't my lucky day," said Philipippa, patting the broom affectionately. "We are going to be great friends, I can see."

Next day, quite early, a crotchety old woman came knocking on the Royal Kitchen door. Philipippa had almost finished all her sweeping for the morning, so the cook was about to set her scrubbing. But first she had to answer the door.

"May I ask what you are doing with my broom?" snapped the crotchety old woman.

"*Your* broom?" cried Philipippa in astonishment. "Why, I bought it myself in the market yesterday."

"What if you did?" said the crotchety old woman. "I tell you it is my broom, just the same," and she tried to snatch it away.

"Well, and what about me?" the broom asked suddenly, in a swishy-swooshy voice.

Philipippa was so surprised that

she let go of the broom handle with a jerk. It didn't fall, but stood all by itself in the middle of the floor!

"Come here at once!" cackled the crotchety old woman. "How dare you run away like that?"

"Run away yourself," piped the broom, "you crusty old cross-patch! I am much happier where I am, thank you."

73

"Oh, are you?" cried the old woman. "We'll soon see who is the boss around here."

"Oh, shall we?" retorted the broom, quivering with rage. "Go away at once, or I'll sweep you out!"

"Oh, you mustn't do that," said Philipippa.

But no sooner had she spoken than the broom began sweeping as hard as it could go. It swept the old woman out of the kitchen, across the courtyard and over the palace drawbridge. *Swish, swish, swish!*

The cook came running to see what was the matter.

Swish, swish, swish, went the broom! *Pop, pop, pop,* went the cook's buttons! She burst right out of her dress and went running away in her petticoat.

And then, all of a sudden, the broom was back in Philipippa's hand, just as if nothing had happened.

The cook and the crotchety old woman didn't come back, so Philipippa kept the wonder broom. And though she never told anyone the tale, no one ever bullied her again!

The Hedley Kow

Maggie Pearson

What sort of creature is the Hedley Kow? It's not a cow, that's for sure – well, only sometimes. Sometimes it looks like a cow.

Sometimes like a horse – and a very fine horse, too, until you try to ride it. Then it's likely to turn itself into a bale of straw, or a pool of water, or . . . You may see the Hedley Kow and never know it:

who's to say?

There was an old woman who made ends meet as best she could. A bit of sewing here. A bit of apple-picking there. A bit of mowing in some other place. It was a hard life, but she made the best of it.

One day while she was walking home, she spied what looked like an old cooking-pot lying in the ditch.

"Well!" she said. "There's a lucky thing! I daresay the pot has a hole in it, or it wouldn't have been thrown away, but it's just the thing to stand on my window-ledge with a pot of flowers inside it." She went and looked at the pot more closely.

It was full of
gold pieces.

"Well!" she
said. "That is
a lucky
thing! It's a
case of finders
keepers, I
suppose. I shall be able to live in
comfort for the rest of my days."

The pot of gold was too heavy to
carry, so she tied her shawl around
it and began to drag it home.

Even then it was hard work, and
after a while she had to stop and
rest. She looked inside the pot
again.

"Well!" she said. "It's not gold after all, it's silver. That's luckier still. I shouldn't have been happy with all that gold about the house. There's thieves and there's beggars and there's the neighbours getting jealous. I'll be much better off with silver."

Off she went again, with her shawl tied round the pot, dragging it along behind her.

It wasn't long before she had to stop and rest again.

She went to look at the silver in the pot, and found it wasn't a pot at all, but a solid lump of iron.

"Well!" said the old woman. "I do get luckier and luckier still! I'd never have known what to do with all that silver, for I've never had more than one silver sixpence at a time in all my life before. But a lump of iron is just what I've been needing to prop my door open, so that the sun can shine straight in."

Off she went again, with her shawl wrapped around the lump of iron, dragging it behind her. She didn't stop until she came to her own front door.

Then she bent down to untie the shawl. As soon as she had done so, the lump of iron shook itself, stood up on four long legs, gave a laugh and went galloping off into the dark.

"Well!" said the old woman. "Isn't that the luckiest thing of all! If I hadn't brought home that old iron pot – that turned out to be full of gold – that turned out to be silver – that turned out to be a lump of iron – I'd never have seen the Hedley Kow with these two eyes of mine. I must be the luckiest old woman alive."

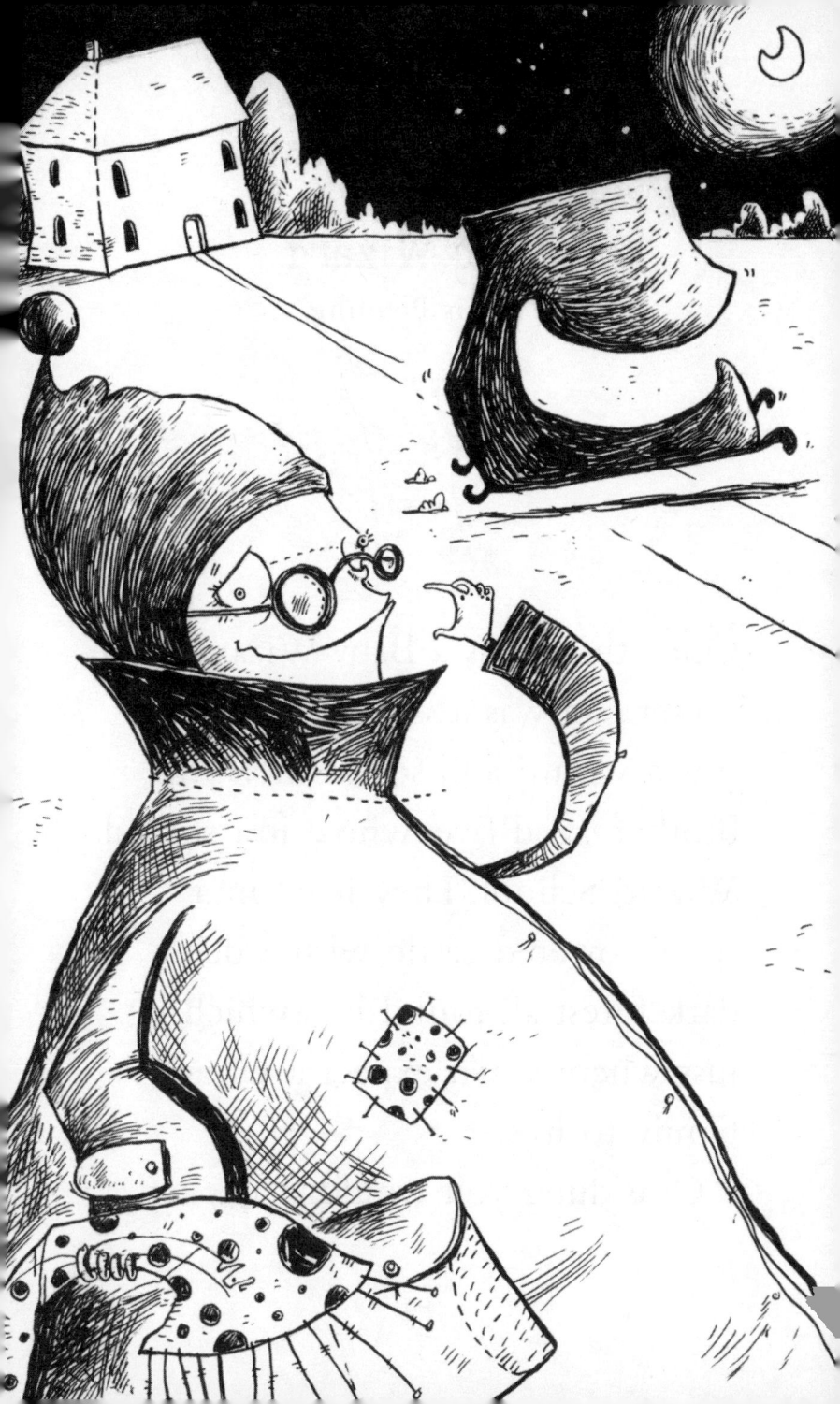

Baby Wizard

Chris Powling

Once there was a Baby Wizard.

Her dad was a wizard, her mum was a wizard and so was her big brother, aged five, who'd just started Wizard School. They lived in a spiky-towered castle with a deep, dark forest all round it – which is just where you'd expect a wizard family to live.

One thing you wouldn't expect,

Baby Wizard

though. This Baby Wizard was special. She couldn't walk yet. She couldn't talk yet. She couldn't feed herself yet − and she certainly couldn't use her potty.

BUT SHE COULD MAKE MAGIC!

At first, of course, the family didn't believe it.

"Impossible," said her dad.

"Wizards must *learn* how to make magic – no one can be magical while they're still wearing a nappy!"

Baby Wizard could.

"Goo-goo-goo," she said. And instantly she turned her pram into a racing car that roared straight down the motorway as far as the big city. Her mum and dad were furious when they had to collect her from the police station.

Mealtimes were even worse. Sometimes Baby Wizard turned her food into rubber so it bounced all over the castle kitchen. Sometimes she made it so heavy it fell to the floor with a CRASH that shook

the whole forest. Sometimes she
floated it out of the window, so it
hung high over the castle like a
tiny, food-coloured cloud.

At bathtimes she was even
naughtier – filling the bath with
crocodiles, for instance.

"Crocodiles?" shrieked Mum,
snatching Baby Wizard from the
water. "She's too little even to have
heard of crocodiles!"

"Goo-goo-goo," said Baby Wizard. And the crocodiles changed into dragons so fiery they nearly burnt the bathroom to bits with their breath.

Naturally, all this was a great nuisance – but nothing more than a nuisance. Remember, every member of her family was a wizard. They could always put things right with plenty of magic of their own.

The real problem came at bedtime.

Bedtime, yes.

Her mum and dad and her big brother, aged five, were too terrified now to go to sleep. Night after night they lay awake, wondering what Baby Wizard would get up to after dark.

"Suppose it's a magic sneeze!" exclaimed her dad. "She might blow away the whole forest!"

"Suppose it's a magic burp!" cried Mum. "She might split the castle in two like an earthquake!"

"Suppose it's a magic nightmare!" yelled her big brother, aged five. "She might fill every corner of the forest with gho-gho-gho-ghosts!"

Even when they took turns to watch over Baby Wizard's cot, it didn't help. They were still so scared of what might happen none of them shut their eyes for a moment.

"This is terrible," yawned Baby Wizard's Mum. "I can't remember when we last had a good night's sleep."

"We're falling to bits from tiredness," Dad groaned. "Isn't there anything we can do?"

Baby Wizard's big brother, aged

five, looked down at his little sister
in her cot and scratched his head
thoughtfully.

"Dad," he said. "Can
a kitten do magic?"

"A kitten?"

"Or a puppy?"

"A puppy?"

"Or a chick?
Or a calf? Or a
piglet?"

"Of course not,"
Dad Wizard said.
"Only a wizard can do
magic – you learn how at Wizard
School. Or so I thought, until your
sister came along."

"That's what I thought," said Baby Wizard's big brother, aged five. "So now I've got the answer to our problem!"

Quickly he waggled his fingers and muttered a magic word.

"Miaow-miaow-miaow," went Baby Wizard in her sleep. Then, "Purr-purr-purr."

Baby Wizard's big brother, aged five, had turned her into a kitten!

Every bedtime after that, Baby Wizard licked her whiskers, curled her tail and purred herself to sleep till morning . . . except, of course, when she'd been turned into a puppy or a chick or a calf or a piglet.

And her family slept happily ever after.

Especially her big brother, aged five, who'd just started Wizard School. Some people say that by the time he's grown up he'll be the best wizard ever . . . unless, of course, his sister is just as good.

The Queen of the Bees

Vivian French

Once there were three sisters who lived in a fine big castle. Their father was a king and their mother was a queen, so all three were princesses – and very special the two eldest thought themselves.

"Of course," the eldest princess said, "I am as beautiful as the moon!"

"HUH!" said the second princess.

"YOU? Why, I am as beautiful as the sun!"

"What RUBBISH!" said the eldest, and she stamped her foot.

"EVERYBODY knows I am the most beautiful!"

"PIFFLE!" shouted the second. "Absolute PIFFLE!"

The king listened, and he shook his head sadly. The queen tut-tutted to herself. The Prime Minister snorted.

"If you'll excuse me saying so, Your Majesties," he said, "I think it's high time those princesses went out on a quest. They'll never find a prince any other way – they're too rude."

"POOH!" said the two princesses. "We don't want to do that!"

The youngest princess was helping

a butterfly escape
out of the window.
"What's a quest?" she
asked.

"You're a ninny!" said her eldest
sister. "Fancy not knowing that!
It's going out on an adventure to
find your fortune!"

"And breaking a spell and finding
a prince," said the second princess.
"But you're MUCH too stupid ever
to do that."

"Yes," said the eldest, "MUCH
too stupid!"

The Prime Minister coughed.
"Excuse me, Your Majesties, but
doesn't that rather prove my point?"

The king sighed heavily. "You're quite right," he said. "But is a quest the only way?"

The Prime Minister nodded. "Yes," he said. "Unless you want them here in the palace for ever and ever."

The king and the queen looked horrified.

"A quest it shall be," said the king.

"At once!" said the queen.

The three princesses were sent off on their quest the very next day. The two eldest moaned and complained bitterly, but the king and queen were firm.

"You can come back as soon as you've finished," said the king.

"As soon as you've found your fortune and broken a spell and found your prince," said the queen. "I'm sure it won't take long." And she waved them goodbye from the top of the castle.

The two eldest princesses walked slowly down the road, huffing and puffing. The youngest danced in front of them, singing happily. Gradually the road grew more and more winding, and they found themselves in a strange land where the trees were bent and twisted and the grass was dry and dusty. The sun was going down, and the sisters began to yawn.

"Time to stop," said the eldest. She pushed the youngest. "Hurry up and find some sticks. We need a fire to keep us warm. I'm going to have a rest." She was about to sit down when the second sister screamed.

"Eek! Don't sit there! Look at all those HORRID little ants!"

"YUCK!" The eldest jumped up.

"Let's squish them and squash them!"

"NO!"

The youngest came running up. "Poor little ants!"

The eldest sister stared for a moment. Then she grinned. "All right. But only if you make us an ENORMOUS fire. AND find us something to eat! AND make us great big comfy beds!"

"That's right," said the second. "Because if you don't, we'll squash and squish EVERY SINGLE ant!"

The youngest daughter scurried about. She built a fire, and she found

sweet berries and nuts, and piled soft
bracken and thistledown into beds
for her two sisters. When the two
princesses were fast asleep and snoring
loudly, she sat down with a sigh.

"Thank you, Princess," said a
teeny tiny voice.

The youngest princess looked
all around. There was a tickle on
her arm, and she saw an ant
standing there, bowing.

"Thank you for your kindness. If
ever you have need of help, call for
the King of the Ants, and I will
help you!"

The two elder sisters were late getting up the next day. They said it was the youngest's fault for making their beds too soft, and they began arguing about where they should begin to look for fortunes and spells and princes.

"There certainly won't be anything around here," said the eldest. "There's nothing but boring old bushes and trees."

"No," agreed the second. "And boring old rushes and reeds."

"Rushes?" said the youngest. "Then there must be a stream!" And she ran to look.

"QUACK! QUACK!" A duck

flew up into the air from under her feet. A flurry of ducklings scattered and hopped into the stream that was hidden under the bushes.

"QUICK!" shouted the eldest sister. "Catch them! We can have delicious duck for breakfast!"

"And duckling pie for supper!" said the second.

"NO! NO!" said the youngest sister. "Dear little ducklings!"

Her two sisters stopped and looked at each other.

"Hmm," said the eldest. "What will you do for us if we leave the ducks alone?"

"I'll make you breakfast! And supper! And soft, comfy beds!"

"Well . . . " said the second.

"I PROMISE!" said the youngest.

When the two eldest sisters had eaten their breakfast they lay down again. The youngest princess sat beside the stream, watching the fluffy yellow ducklings bobbing on the ripples.

"QUACK!" said a duck, stepping out of the reeds. "Thank you,

Princess. If ever you need my help, just call for the King of the Ducks!"

By the end of the day, all three princesses were tired and hungry. They walked away from the stream and up and over a hill, and their feet were sore and their clothes were dusty.

"I can't walk a step further," said the eldest princess.

"Nor me," said the second, and

they flumped down on the
ground under a tall tree. The
youngest sat down too, but her
sisters pulled her hair.

"We want our supper!"
they demanded. "And we
want it NOW!"

The youngest got slowly to her
feet. There was a faint buzzing, and
they all looked up. Hanging from a
branch of the tree right above them
was a bees' nest.

"HONEY!"
The eldest princess began shaking
the branch. The bees buzzed angrily.

"HONEY!" said the second, and
she shook the youngest sister.

"Quick!
Climb up
and fetch us
the honey!
Beat the nest
down! Do it
NOW!"

"NO! NO! NO!" said the youngest. "Leave the bees! Please leave the bees!"

But her sisters would not listen to her. They hurried to fetch long sticks, and came crashing back through the wood waving them.

"NO!" said the youngest. "NO!" And she climbed up the tree and held the bees' nest in her arms.

Bees flew all around her, but not one stung her.

The two eldest sisters looked at each other, and threw down their sticks.

"You'd better promise us something VERY special," said the second.

"VERY special indeed!" said the eldest.

"I'll find the fortunes!" promised the youngest princess. "I'll break the spells! I'll find the princes!"

"Very well," said the eldest sister. "But you'd better be quick about it!"

"That's right," said the second.

"We're TIRED of questing!"

That night, the youngest sister could not sleep. She climbed right up to the top of the tree, and looked out over the starlit land. The bees hummed about her, and a small voice buzzed in her ear.

"Thank you, Princess! Thank you! If ever you have need of us, call for the Queen of the Bees!"

The youngest sister smiled. "I'll remember." She climbed a little higher, and stopped. What was that she could see outlined against the night sky? She rubbed her eyes. It looked like a castle . . .

The two eldest sisters were not pleased at being woken up.

"Quick!" called the youngest sister. "I can see a castle! It must be the end of our quest!"

The three princesses reached the castle as the sun began to rise. The eldest knocked loudly on the door, and a little old woman opened it.

"We've come to find our fortunes and break the spells and rescue the

princes, old hag!" said the eldest
princess rudely.

"So let us in!" said the second.
The old woman
nodded. She led them
inside, and showed them
a courtyard full of tall
grass and weeds.
All around were
stone statues . . .
statues of
princesses. They looked
surprised and angry —
and very, very still.

"Excuse me," said the
youngest princess, "but
what are these?"

The old woman cackled. "Princesses, my dear," she said. "Come a-questing they did, but they couldn't break the spell. The spell caught them instead!"

The two eldest princesses took a step back, and pushed the youngest forward. "SHE'S going to do the spell-breaking," they said. "SHE'S the one who'll get turned into stone if she fails!"

The little old woman cackled again. "Too late, my dears! If she fails, you ALL get turned into stone!"

The two eldest turned around to run, but the door was firmly shut.

They glared at the youngest. "You'd better get it right!"

The youngest sighed. "Where do I begin?"

The little old woman pointed to the grassy courtyard.

"Hidden in here are a thousand pearls," she said. "Find them all, and that's your fortune. Fail, and you'll be turned to stone!"

"And then?" asked the youngest.

The little old woman took her arm. "Look here," she said.

The youngest daughter looked down and saw a deep dark well, full of gleaming water.

"At the bottom is a golden key," said the old woman. "Find it, or you'll all be turned to stone."

"And then?" asked the youngest.

The old woman rubbed her hands together. "Then we'll see what we'll see! But you'll never find the key!" And she shuffled away.

The two eldest princesses sat down and burst into tears.

"We don't want to be turned to stone!" they wailed. "We want to

go HOME!"
The youngest
took no notice.
She sat down among the poppies
and daisies, and called, "King of
the Ants! King of the Ants!
I need you!"

Almost at once there was
a faint rustling from
among the long grasses
as ants came hurrying
and scurrying from all around. They
came in twos and threes
and fours, and
carried with
them the
shimmering pearls.

The youngest daughter sat and counted, and in only an hour all the pearls were heaped at her feet.

"Thank you, thank you!" she called as the ants scurried away.

The old woman was not pleased at the youngest princess's success. She grunted as she took her to the well, but the princess smiled as she knelt down beside the water.

"King of the Ducks! King of the Ducks! I need you!"

QUAAAAAAAAAAAACK!

There was a flurry and flapping of wings, and the King of the Ducks landed with a loud splash. He winked at the youngest princess, and dived deep deep down into the well. In no time, she had the dripping golden key on her lap.

"Thank you, thank you, King of the Ducks!" she called as the duck beat his wings and flew away.

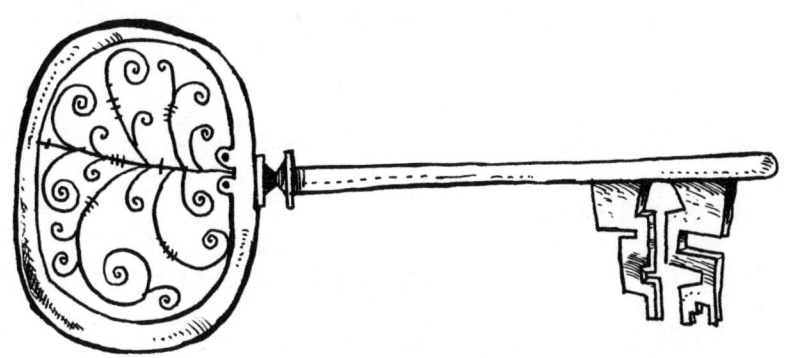

The old woman took the key. "You must come this way," she said, and unlocked a huge golden door. The youngest princess followed her, and the two eldest princesses came behind, snuffling.

Behind the golden door was a huge golden hall, and in the hall was a great stone bed. Lying in the bed were three princes, as like one another as three peas.

The two eldest princesses clapped their hands as they looked.

"So HANDSOME!" whispered the eldest.

The second sister pinched the youngest. "Wake them up!"

The old woman cackled again. "Not so fast! Stone they are, and stone you'll be if you choose wrong!" She turned to the youngest princess. "One ate sugar, one ate syrup, and the youngest ate honey before they were enchanted! Now, choose the youngest!"

The youngest princess walked slowly over to the bed.

"Queen of the Bees!" she whispered. "Queen of the Bees!"

There was a gentle humming, and in through the open window zigzagged the Queen of the Bees.

She flew over the three princes, and settled on the nearest. The youngest princess sat down on the bed and put out her hand.

"This is the youngest prince!" she said.

At once there was a rush of wind, and the sound of hurrying feet and chattering voices as the stone princesses leapt back into life. They burst into the golden hall, but as they did so the bed gave a hop and a skip and a jump and soared up and out of the window. The two eldest princesses were only just in time to snatch at the covers and hang on tightly.

The king and the queen and the Prime Minister were walking in the royal garden when the bed landed with a THUMP! beside them. The two eldest princesses picked themselves up and dusted themselves down. The youngest was still sitting on the bed, holding the hand of the youngest prince. They were smiling happily at each other.

"Well, well!" said the Prime Minister. "Welcome back!"

"We've found our fortunes!" said the eldest princess, and she tipped the thousand pearls out of her pockets.

"AND our princes!" said the second, pointing to the bed.

The two eldest princes sat up and bowed.

"So glad to meet you," they said, and lay down again.

"Aren't they HANDSOME?" said the eldest princess proudly.

"Indeed we are," said the eldest prince. "We are as handsome as the moon and the sun together!"

"Exactly so," said the second prince. "And now – bring us our breakfasts!"

125

The King of the Blue Lagoon
Ann Turnbull

When Sally was at the seaside, she found a stone on the beach. It was grey and oval and smoothed by the waves and it just filled the palm of her hand. Sally knew at once that it was a magic stone. She kept it in her pocket.

One day when Sally was skipping in the school playground the stone bounced out of her pocket and fell – plop! – into a puddle.

The puddle changed. It changed from a grey rainy-day puddle to a pool of deep, deep blue, with pink rocks in it, and glinting fish that flicked between them. Sally heard the boom and hiss of the surf. She put her hand into the water. It was warm and she felt a tickle of fish. Her stone lay at the bottom. Sally took it out, and at once the blue sea, the surf, the pink rocks and glinting fish all vanished. And from Sally's hand came a voice that sighed:

"Far from the coral caves

Far from the sea

A witch's magic has enchanted me."

Sally put the stone back in her pocket. She looked around. No one else had noticed.

When she got home, she took the stone into the garden. In the garden was a pond, with rocks around the edge and a plastic gnome fishing at the side.

Sally put the stone into the pond.

The water turned deep, deep blue,

the rocks became a coral reef, the gnome turned into a mermaid who combed her hair and sang wild songs.

Sally took the stone out.

The blue sea, the coral reef and the mermaid all vanished and Sally heard a voice that sighed:

"Far from the coral caves
Far from the sea
A witch's magic has enchanted me."

That night, Sally put the stone into her bath.

The bath water turned deep, deep blue. The bath foam turned to sea foam. The soap became an angel fish. The flannel became a manta ray. An island with palm trees grew out of the soap dish. On Sally's plastic boat a pirate crew hoisted the Jolly Roger. Sally launched a Spanish galleon, laden with gold. There was a battle and cannon boomed across the water.

And all the time the stone lay at the bottom of the bath, and Sally's mother hadn't noticed anything.

Sally took the stone out. At once the blue sea, the angel fish, the Spaniards and pirates all vanished and she heard a voice that sighed:

"Far from the coral caves

Far from the sea

A witch's magic has enchanted me."

After that, Sally always put the stone into her bath. But although the water changed and the boats changed and the soap and soap dish changed, the stone never changed. It lay on the bottom, cold and sad, and when Sally took it out, it always sighed:

"Far from the coral caves

Far from the sea

A witch's magic has enchanted me."

One day Sally went to the seaside again. She took the stone with her.

Sally waded into the sea, holding the stone in her cupped hands. She squatted, and the sea washed over the stone and rocked it against her fingers.

The sea was a grey, cold sea. Sally thought it would change, but it didn't. Nothing changed. The sea was grey; the rocks were grey; the sky was grey.

But suddenly, in Sally's hands, the stone came alive. It twitched.

It wiggled.
It slithered
and slipped.
Sally looked
down and
saw that the stone had changed into
a fish: a bright, bright fish with a
rose-red body and turquoise stripes,
golden eyes with black rims, fins
that flicked silver and a rose-red
shimmering tail. On its head was a
crown.

"Oh!" said Sally. She was so
surprised that she opened her
fingers and the fish slipped through.

Before she could catch it, it
flicked its tail and wiggled its body

and swam away, bright as a jewel in the grey sea. Sally watched it grow smaller and smaller until at last it was no bigger than a sequin. Then it disappeared.

Sally felt something scraping and bumping against her foot. She bent down and picked up a shell. It was a big shell, pale pink and spiralled, that looked as if it had come from a blue sea far away. Sally waded back to the shore, holding her shell.

She knew at once that it was a magic shell. She showed it to her mother.

"You can hear the sea in a shell," said Sally's mother.

Sally held the shell to her ear. She heard the sea. She heard the boom and hiss of far-off surf. And above the sound of the surf she heard a glad voice, singing:

"Deep in the coral caves
Under the sea
King of the Blue Lagoon
now I am free."

Tom Thumb

Joyce Dunbar

A woodcutter was chopping logs in his yard while his wife threw corn to the chickens. "If only we had a child to play around us," he said, "then we should be really happy."

"I couldn't agree more," said his wife. "Why, if I could have one small son, even no bigger than my thumb, I should be the happiest woman alive."

Now it so happened that the fairies heard them and decided to grant their wish. Not long after, the wood-cutter's wife had a tiny child, not much bigger than her thumb. He could walk and talk in no time and the fairies made him a suit of clothes. His hat was made of an oak leaf, his shirt spun out of spiders' webs, his jacket woven from thistledown, and his trousers from feathers.

His mother and father were overjoyed. "We have got what we wished for," they said, "and we will always love him dearly." They called him Tom Thumb.

Even though he was so little, he was as merry and mischievous as any child could be. "Can I help you plough the fields, Father?" he asked one day.

"Why no, you are much too small to ride a horse, Tom," said his father.

"Oh no I'm not," said Tom. "Just set me in the horse's ear." His father did so. "Whoa," said Tom, and "Steady," straight into the horse's ear. All went well until Tom decided to go for a gallop. "Gee-up!" he suddenly yelled, so that the horse ran through the town, upskittling all the market stalls in the high street.

"You are a bad lad, Tom Thumb," said his father when he caught up with him. "You will never make your way in the world if you play tricks like that."

Even so, he let Tom ride home in his favourite place, on the rim of his hat, for his son was the apple of his eye.

"Can I help you mix the batter pudding?" Tom asked his mother on another day.

"But, Tom, you are too small," she replied.

"Oh no I'm not," said Tom. "Just set me on the table."

But no sooner was her back turned than Tom decided to go boating on the bowl of batter in half an eggshell.

Tom Thumb

The eggshell upturned, tipping
Tom Thumb into the mixture.
He kicked and thrashed about, and
might have drowned if his mother
hadn't fished him out in time.

"Whatever shall I do with you?"
she said. "I don't see how you will
ever make your way in the world."

Even so, she kissed him and
washed him in a teacup, for her son
was her pride and joy.

Soon after, Tom's mother took
him out milking in the meadow.
He sneaked out of her apron pocket
and ran down a snail shell. "Here I
am!" he called. Then he hid down a
mouse-hole. "Here I am!" he called.

Then he crept under a stone, still calling, "Here I am!"

This time his mother caught him and tied him to a thistle with a fine thread so that she might get on with her milking. But the cow thought she saw a tasty morsel and took Tom and the thistle in one mouthful. Round and round he was tumbled, with the cow's great teeth chewing and grinding. "Here I am, Mother!" he cried out in terror.

"You're a wicked little boy, Tom Thumb," she replied. "I cannot play hide-and-seek all morning." And she went on with her milking.

"Mother, please come and get me!" yelled Tom, so loudly that his voice tickled the cow's tonsils and he was coughed up into the long grass. He began waving his arms so wildly that a raven swept him up and dropped him into the sea, where he was swallowed by an enormous fish.

Luckily, the fish was caught soon after and presented to a king for his supper. What a shock everyone got when out popped Tom Thumb.

The king was delighted with him. He gave him a mouse with a saddle to ride on, and a darning needle for a sword. Tom charged around, scaring spiders away from the three princesses, so that they made him their champion knight.

But Tom was missing his father and mother. "You shall go home to see them," said the king, "and you shall take all the treasure you can carry."

They made him a golden coach

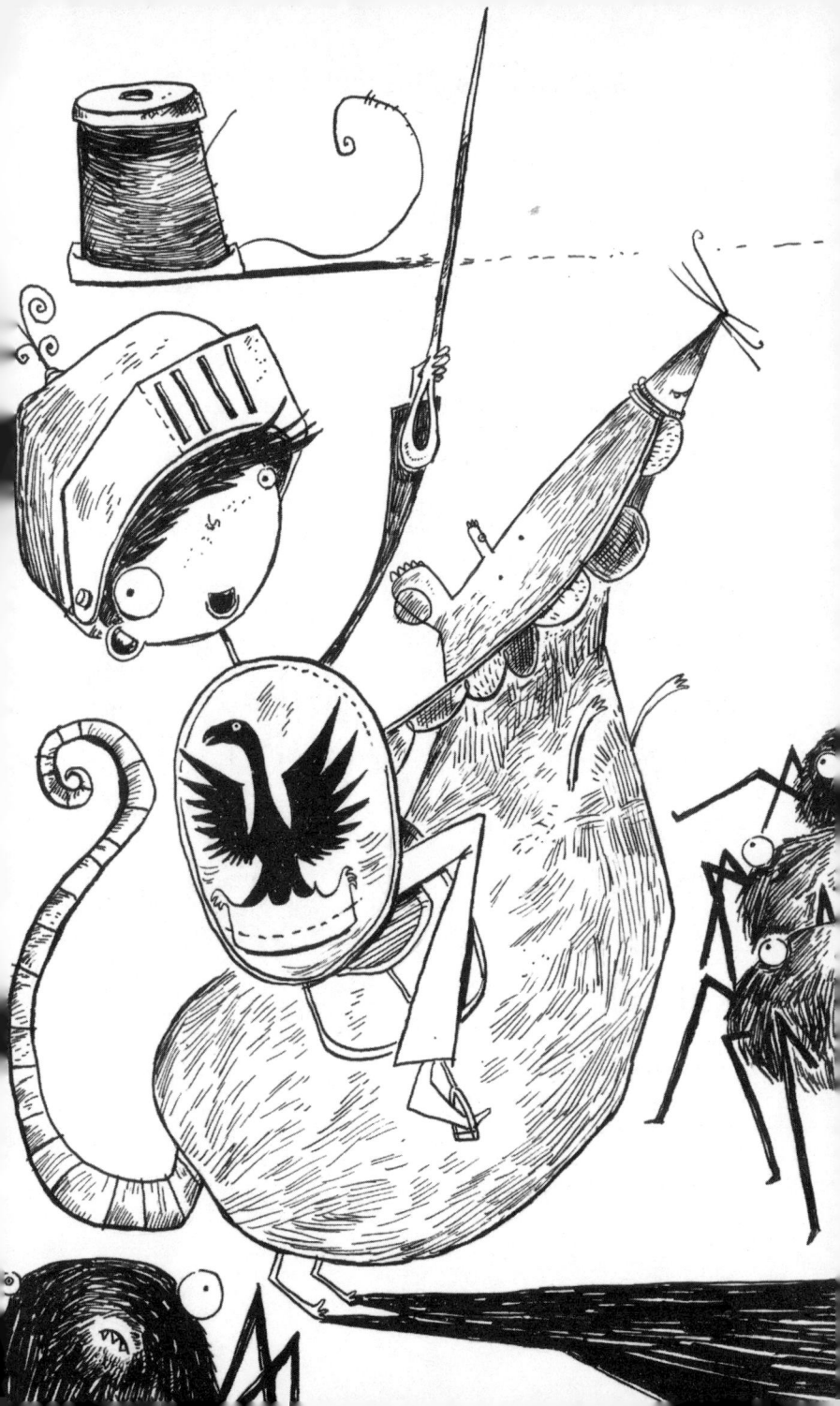

from a walnut shell, with four silver buttons for wheels and six mice to pull it.

Tom set off home with all his treasure, which was a single gold coin. But it took him all day just to reach the edge of the palace grounds. "Not to worry," said the princesses.

"We have some presents from the fairies that will help you to find your way home."

The first

princess gave him an enchanted hat, which shrank to fit the wearer's head, and showed him whatever was going on in all parts of the world. The second gave him a pair of boots, which shrank to fit the wearer's feet, and could in a moment carry him to all corners of the earth. The third gave him a precious ring, which he wore round his waist like a girdle and gave him the strength of a giant.

Tom Thumb put on the hat and saw his mother and father weeping for the loss of him. So he put on the boots and wished that he was home.

"Here I am, Mother!" he cried. "See, Father! I have made my way in the world!"

And to show he had the strength of a giant, he lifted them up in his arms before giving them such a hug!

The Enchanted Princess

Judy Hindley

A beautiful princess named Gloriana was riding in the mountains with her younger sisters. Suddenly, she saw a wonderful deer with eyes like stars . . .

"Catch me if you can!" called the deer.

The princess and her sisters followed the deer. They galloped and galloped as fast as they could go. But however fast they went, the deer was always just ahead.

At last, the poor horses could go no further.

"Let's turn back!" cried Gloriana's sister. But Gloriana wouldn't stop.

Finally, the little sisters could go no further.

"Please turn back!" they called to Gloriana. But even then, she wouldn't stop.

On and on she went, until at last she couldn't even hear their cries.

At that moment, the deer stood still and waited. She ran towards it.

"I am a magician," said the deer. "Do you have any wishes?"

"Oh yes!" cried Gloriana. "I want to be rich and live in a splendid castle with fine new clothes and jewels."

"What about your sisters?" asked the deer. "I heard them calling you."

"Never mind my sisters," said Gloriana. "They're always calling me and running after me. This time, let them find their own way home."

"Very well then," said the deer. "You have your wish. But some day, you will call, and they won't hear.

Oh, my dear, you will cry and cry, until you are as kind as you are beautiful."

Suddenly, the deer was gone, and Gloriana stood on the steps of a shining castle.

That night, Gloriana ate from a golden plate and drank from a golden cup. She went to sleep in a golden bed as big as a boat.

When she woke up, she found rooms full of jewels and rich new clothes. Now she had everything she wanted – but there was no one to see it, and no one to share it with.

Time went by. Soon the splendid castle seemed very lonely.

One day, Gloriana said, "I'll ask my sisters to come and stay with me. They always do what I want."

Away she went along the mountain road.

At last, she saw her sisters in a meadow.

"Sisters, sisters, come with me!" she cried. She jumped off her horse to run to them.

But as soon as her foot touched the ground, she turned into a small, grey rabbit.

"Look! What a dear little rabbit!"
cried her sisters. As they played with
her, she tried to talk to them, but
they couldn't hear a single word.

Just before sunset, they waved
goodbye and went away.

As soon as they had gone,
Gloriana became a princess once
again. But it was too late, she had to
go back alone to her grand castle.

"That mountain must be
bewitched!" said Gloriana. The next
day, away she went, by the river road.

This time, she saw her sisters by
the river-bank.

"Sisters, sisters, come with me!"
she cried.

Again, she jumped off her horse to run to them. But as soon as her foot touched the river-bank, she turned into a little golden fish.

"Look! What a pretty fish!" cried her sisters.

They leaned out over the river to try to see her. She leaped high to try to speak to them. But of course, they couldn't hear a single word.

This time, Gloriana cried and cried, but her tears ran into the river, and no one saw them.

At sunset, her sisters went away. Once again, Gloriana went back alone to her grand castle.

"Perhaps the river is bewitched," said Gloriana. So the next day she rode into the forest.

The forest was dark and gloomy. Gloriana was frightened. But she went on.

Suddenly, the wonderful deer ran across her path. Her sisters came chasing after it with a hunter. They were galloping, galloping, straight towards a cliff.

"Stop, stop!" called Gloriana. She jumped from her horse to stand in front of them. But this time she turned into a great white bear. And when she called, her voice was a great roar.

They stopped – and the hunter raised his bow and shot her.

Down fell the bear, still roaring. As it fell, its roar became the sweet voice of the princess.

The hunter raised his bow to shoot again. But the little princesses heard their sister's voice.

"No!" they cried. "Don't shoot! It's Gloriana!"

They ran to hug the wounded bear and its eyes filled with tears.

Then a voice said, "Don't cry, Gloriana." There stood the wonderful deer with eyes like stars. It said, "You risked your life to save your sisters – you have become as kind as you are beautiful."

And as the deer spoke, Gloriana again became a princess.

Then, suddenly, the deer was gone and the sisters stood on the steps of the shining castle where they stayed together all their long and happy lives.

Acknowledgements

"The Three Wishes", "Tom Thumb" and "The Wonder Broom" reproduced by permission of The Agency (London) Ltd © **Joyce Dunbar** 1993. First published by Kingfisher in *The Kingfisher Read-Aloud Storybook*; "Chantelle, the Princess Who Couldn't Sing" reproduced by permission of The Agency (London) Ltd © **Joyce Dunbar** 1997. First published by Kingfisher in *Breaking the Spell: Tales of Enchantment*; "The Queen of the Bees" taken from *Breaking the Spell: Tales of Enchantment* (Kingfisher) by **Vivian French** copyright © Vivian French 1997; "The Enchanted Princess" and "The Magical Apple Tree" taken from *My Own Fairy Story Book* (Kingfisher) by **Judy Hindley** copyright © Judy Hindley 1991; "The Cletterkin" taken from *Stories for the Very Young* (Kingfisher) by **Jenny Koralek** copyright © Jenny Koralek 1989; "The Hedley Kow" taken from *Time for Telling* (Kingfisher) by **Maggie Pearson** copyright © Maggie Pearson 1991; "Baby Wizard" taken from *Bedtime Stories for the Very Young* (Kingfisher) by **Chris Powling** copyright © Chris Powling 1991; "The King of the Blue Lagoon" taken from *Bedtime Stories for the Very Young* (Kingfisher) by **Ann Turnbull** copyright © Ann Turnbull 1991.